Jennifer of the Jungle

written and illustrated by Corbin Hillam

For my wife Jane

Copyright © 1990 Concordia Publishing House
3558 S. Jefferson Avenue, St. Louis, MO 63118-3968
Manufactured in the United States of America

Library of Congress Cataloging in Publication Data

Hillam, Corbin.
  Jennifer of the jungle/by Corbin Hillam: illustrated by Corbin Hillam.

  Summary: The daughter of missionaries describes how she and her family continue to spread the word of God as they leave their jungle mission and come to the city for a visit.
  ISBN 0-570-04182-1
  1. Missionary stories. 2. Children of missionaries—Juvenile literature. 3. Missionaries—Leaves and furloughs—Juvenile literature. [1. Missionaries.] I. Title.
BV2087.H4852   1990
266—dc20   89-35420
                                                              CIP
                                                               AC

1 2 3 4 5 6 7 8 9 10   99 98 97 96 95 94 93 92 91 90

Hi! My name is Jennifer. Every morning I wake up to the sounds of screeching parrots and chattering monkeys. That's because I live in the jungle. I love my jungle home.

After I say good morning to my jungle friends, I go out on the fron porch and eat breakfast with my family. There is my mom and dad, and my big brother Josh.

After breakfast Josh, Mom, Dad, and I wash the dishes and clean up the house. When we are all done, Dad goes to help some of the people in our village.

Dad is a missionary. He likes to tell people that Jesus loves them. He helps people who are sick, or in trouble, or who just need a friend.

Josh and I walk to school with our friends. Mom is a missionary, too. She stays at home and works on her Bible. Mom is writing God's Word in the language of our villagers. Then they can read the Bible and learn about Jesus just like we do.

After school I love to play with my friends. We explore in the jungle, swim in the river, and collect treasures.

About once a month Skip comes to visit us. He is a pilot. He flies his plane all over the jungle.

We don't have a store or post office in the jungle. Skip flies in everything we need. He brings us extra food, books, medicine, and news from other parts of the jungle.

One time when Josh broke his arm, Skip flew him out to the jungle hospital.

Usually when Skip visits he can only stay for a few minutes. One time he let me sit in the pilot's seat while he unloaded the plane. Skip is a good friend.

Tonight at dinner Dad says, "It's time for us to go home on furlough."

"What's a furlough?" I ask. "And besides, isn't this our home?" I add.

"Every few years missionaries take sort of a vacation," Dad explains. "We call it a furlough. We need to go to where Grandpa lives to visit our friends and family. They want to know how we are doing. And yes, this is our home," Dad says.

Josh seems so excited about leaving and seeing his friends and cousins. I was only one year old when we moved to our jungle home, so don't remember anything else.

At bedtime I ask Mom, "Will we come back here?"

"Yes, Jennifer, we will. But tonight we need to ask Jesus to help us as we travel to Grandpa's house," replies Mom.

I pray, "Dear Jesus, I feel kind of scared to leave my home. Please keep Mom and Dad and Josh and me safe on the airplane. Amen."

Now we have to pack our clothes. We can't take too much because everything needs to fit in Skip's plane for the trip out of the jungle.

This is the day we get to go! I watch the sky all morning. Finally I see Skip's plane. He has brought a new missionary family with him. They will live in our house while we are gone. Dad and Mom show them around while Josh and I help Skip load the plane.

As we fly away, I say good-bye to my jungle home. Below me I can see all my friends. I ask Jesus to take care of my friends while I am gone.

We are in Skip's airplane for more than three hours! I never knew the jungle was so big!

At last we land at an airstrip. There is a town here with stores and even
a church. I can see the hospital that Skip took Josh to when he broke his
arm.

Compared to our village, this town seems like a big city! It's a good
thing Jamie, Skip's son, is here to show me around.

Today we need to get up early. We ride the bus all day to get to the international airport. For part of the time Josh rides on the roof of the bus. What an adventure!

Finally we get to the city. Another missionary meets us and takes us to the airport. We are going to ride in a huge jet plane to Grandpa's house. I've never seen anything so big!

The plane ride is great! I eat two meals, watch a movie, and even go to the bathroom! Skip's plane is nothing like this. But then, I guess it would be hard to land a jet plane in the jungle.

Finally the plane lands. Everyone is there to meet us—Grandpa and Grandma, my aunts and uncles, and all my cousins. Too bad I don't know any of them. Boy, am I tired!

We all get to ride in Grandpa's big car to his house. The city seems so big! "Mom," I ask, "will I hear the parrots in the morning?" The next thing I know I'm being put in a strange bed.

When I finally wake up it's the next afternoon. I think I slept for a whole day. I look out the window and all I see are houses.

Going downstairs I find Dad, Mom, Grandpa, Grandma, and Josh all in the living room. "Grandpa," I say, "I want to climb some trees."

But nobody hears me. They are all busy talking about seeing their friends and going shopping. I miss my jungle.

Finally, all I can to do is go outside and sit on Grandpa's front porch. Suddenly a kid pokes her head up from some bushes. "Want to play?" she asks.

"Sure!" I say. And off we run. First we go to the playground. My new
iend Corrie shows me the swings and merry-go-round. There is even a
ngle gym! Imagine that!

We sit by the duck pond. I love to hear the ducks quack at me. The
Corrie buys me an ice cream cone. Wow! Is it good!

I tell Corrie that my dad and mom are missionaries. "What's a issionary?" asks Corrie.

"A missionary is somebody who tells about God's love," I say. "Go[d] loves us so much He sent His Son Jesus to die on the cross for us. If w[e] believe in Jesus, we will go to heaven."

"Wow!" Corrie says. "I'd like to know more about Jesus."

What do you know! I'm a missionary, too! How about you? Can you be a missionary today?